# LOUDMOUTH

## George *and the* Cornet

# LOUDMOUTH

## George *and the* Cornet

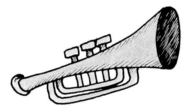

### *Nancy Carlson*

 **Carolrhoda Books, Inc.** ♦ **Minneapolis**

for Kathy Mack, who called *Carolrhoda* for me

*This book is available in two editions:*
Library binding by Carolrhoda Books, Inc.
Soft cover by First Avenue Editions
c/o The Lerner Group
241 First Avenue North
Minneapolis, Minnesota 55401

LIBRARY OF CONGRESS CATALOGING IN PUBLICATION DATA

**Carlson, Nancy L.**
  Loudmouth George and the cornet.

  Summary: George's cornet playing is too much for both
his family and the band.
  [1. Rabbits—Fiction. 2. Cornet—Fiction. 3. Bands
(Music)—Fiction.]  I. Title.
PZ7.C21665Ln   1983        [E]            82-22171
ISBN 0-87614-214-5

Manufactured in the United States of America
4  5  6  7  8  9  –  P/JP  –  02  01  00  99  98  97

CORNET

George got a lot of presents for his birthday, but his very favorite came from Uncle Chuck. It was a brand new, shiny, brass cornet.

"Oh, boy!" said George. "I'm going to be a star!"

George played his cornet every day for a week.

By Saturday he thought he was really good.

"Hey, Mother," he said, "listen to me play 'Moon River.'"

"Pretty good, huh?" said George when he'd finished.

Mother didn't say a word.

I must be even better than I think, thought
George. I left her speechless! It's time I had
a bigger audience.

On Monday George joined the school band.

"All of our members take lessons after school," said Mr. Sharp, the band director. "Let's see, I can fit you in on Mondays at 4:30."

"That sounds like a lot of work," said George. "Besides, I don't need lessons. I'm already great."

"Well, we'll try you out for a week then," said Mr. Sharp.

On Tuesday George went to his first rehearsal. Most of the members were just learning to play their instruments. George was a little annoyed.

Mr. Sharp had them warm up by playing scales.

Then he directed them on "Three Blind Mice."

"This is pretty boring stuff," said George to Harriet, who sat next to him. "Why don't you come over to my house after school and I'll teach you how to play 'Moon River.'"

"No thanks," said Harriet.

On Wednesday Tony was practicing his
flute.

"Isn't that beautiful," sighed Harriet.

"I don't think he quite has it," said George.
"Here, Tony, let me show you how it's done."

"That band has a lot to learn," George
told his family that evening.

Then he went upstairs to play "Moon River."

On Thursday Mr. Sharp asked the class
if anyone would like to play a solo.

"I would! I would!" said George.

"How about you, Harriet?" said Mr. Sharp.

"That was very good," said Mr. Sharp
when Harriet had finished. "Anyone else?"
"Me! Me! Let me play!" said George.
"How about you, Ralph?" said Mr. Sharp.

"Very nice," said Mr. Sharp when Ralph was through.

"Let me! Let me!" yelled George. "I want to play now."

"Oh, all right, George," said Mr. Sharp.

I'll give them a real treat, thought George.

On Friday Mr. Sharp asked George to
stay after practice.

"George," he said, "I'm afraid I'm going
to have to ask you to quit the band."

"Quit!" said George. "But what will you do without me?"

When George got home he told his mother
the news.
"Oh, George," she said, "I'm so sorry."

"Never mind, Mother," said George. "That band was pretty crummy, and I was getting a little tired of playing the cornet anyway...."

I'm going to take up the tuba instead!"